The Fort

written and photographed
by
Mia Coulton

Danny's Big Adventure #5

The Fort

Published by:
MaryRuth Books, Inc.
18660 Ravenna Road
Chagrin Falls, OH 44023

www.maryruthbooks.com

Text copyright © 2011 Mia Coulton
Photographs copyright © 2011 Mia Coulton

Editor: Heidi Makela

Library of Congress Control Number: 2010918760
ISBN 978-1-933624-71-6

Printed in the United States of America
10 9 8 7 6 5 4 3 2 1
First Edition

SPC/0111/20543

For Elizabeth, Robert and Kathleen

Contents

Fall

It was fall.

The leaves on the trees were

beginning to change color.

Danny loved fall.

He loved to sniff the ground.

Sometimes he would find

an apple.

Then he would eat it.

He loved to see

all the pumpkins

in the pumpkin patch.

Sometimes he would pick one.

Then he would eat it.

He loved to run

in the cornfield.

He would pick an ear of corn.

He would eat that, too!

But most of all,

Danny loved to play outside

with his toy, Bee.

Sometimes they would play

all day in the woods.

It was a sunny fall day.

Danny and Bee were taking

a walk in the woods.

Danny was doing the walking.

Bee was riding up on top.

Danny stopped and looked up.

"One, two, three, four, five, six!

I can count six geese

flying south!"

Danny shouted.

Danny thought, "I am so glad
bees don't fly south.
I would be lonely without
my Bee."

Danny and Bee continued their walk in the woods.

All you could hear was the "crunch, crunch, crunch" of the leaves beneath Danny's paws.

Making a Fort

Danny saw rocks, leaves, and
sticks in the woods.

"Let's make a fort,"
he said to Bee.
"I will fetch some sticks and put
them over the rocks for a roof.
The leaves will make a soft place
for us to lie down.
This will be our fort
in the woods."

Danny looked around to see
where he could put Bee.

He saw a spot by a tree.
He put Bee down beside the tree
and said, "You stay here while
I go make our fort.
I will be back soon."

Danny found short sticks.

He found long sticks.

He found lots and lots of sticks.

He put the sticks on top

of the rocks to make a roof.

He put some leaves under the

roof for a soft place to lie down.

"Just right," he thought.

"A just right fort for a dog

and his toy, Bee."

Danny started to walk back to the tree where he left Bee.

A Lost Bee

Danny went back to the tree

where he left Bee.

He looked in front of the tree.

Bee was not there.

He looked behind the tree.

Bee was not there.

He sat for a moment

and thought, "Is this the spot?

Is this the tree

where I left Bee?

Did Bee go looking for me?"

Danny barked, "Bee! Bee!

Here I am but where are you?"

He looked in a big hole

in the ground.

"Bee! Bee!

Are you down there?"

All he found in the hole was

a grumpy groundhog.

"Excuse me," he said to the

grumpy groundhog.

He saw a hole in a tree.

Danny wondered,

"Did Bee go in there?"

He did not hear buzzing.

"No buzzing, no Bee."

A Found Bee

In the distance,

he saw something

yellow and black resting

by a tree.

It was Bee!

Danny gave a big sigh of relief.

"You really scared me, Bee.

Don't ever get lost again."

He gently picked up Bee.

Danny and Bee sat in their fort.

A dog and his toy, Bee,

they were as happy as could be.